First Edition.
ISBN: Hardback 978-1-950574-15-5
Softback 978-1-950574-16-2

Library of Congress Control Number Applied For

JUV023000 JUVENILE FICTION / Lifestyles / City & Town Life
JUV019000 JUVENILE FICTION / Humorous Stories
JUV039060 JUVENILE FICTION / Social Themes / Friendship

Questions? Comments? We love feedback: info@vestralingua.com

Need information about licensing, custom editions, bulk sales, or academic/corporate purchases? Write the publisher at the address below.

VESTRA LINGUA KIDS
C/o Vestra Lingua LLC
PO Box 2594
West Columbia, SC 29171

www.VestraLingua.com

The Adventures of Andy Dandy
"Andy Dandy's Candy"

Written by
William Savage

—To my grandparents and my 5 children:

Thank you for always showing me the way
and pushing me to be a better storyteller.

W.S.

This story is about a little boy named Andy Dandy. He lives with his mother, father, and little sister. They live in a small town called Sprinkleville. Everybody knows everybody, and there's always something fun to do. Every year, Sprinkleville holds a huge festival with dozens of floats.

The best thing about the parade is all the candy! Sprinkleville is famous for its multi-flavored candy. Andy's dad works at the candy factory, and they make the best candy in the world. The best I tell you.

Every day before Andy went to school, he would pack his backpack with pieces of his favorite candy while his mom fixed his lunch.

After breakfast, Andy would have a piece, and every week, Dad would bring home a new batch of candy. Andy's mom and dad would always say how important it is o share. Sharing is caring, they'd always say. At school, all the kids liked Andy because he would always share his candy.

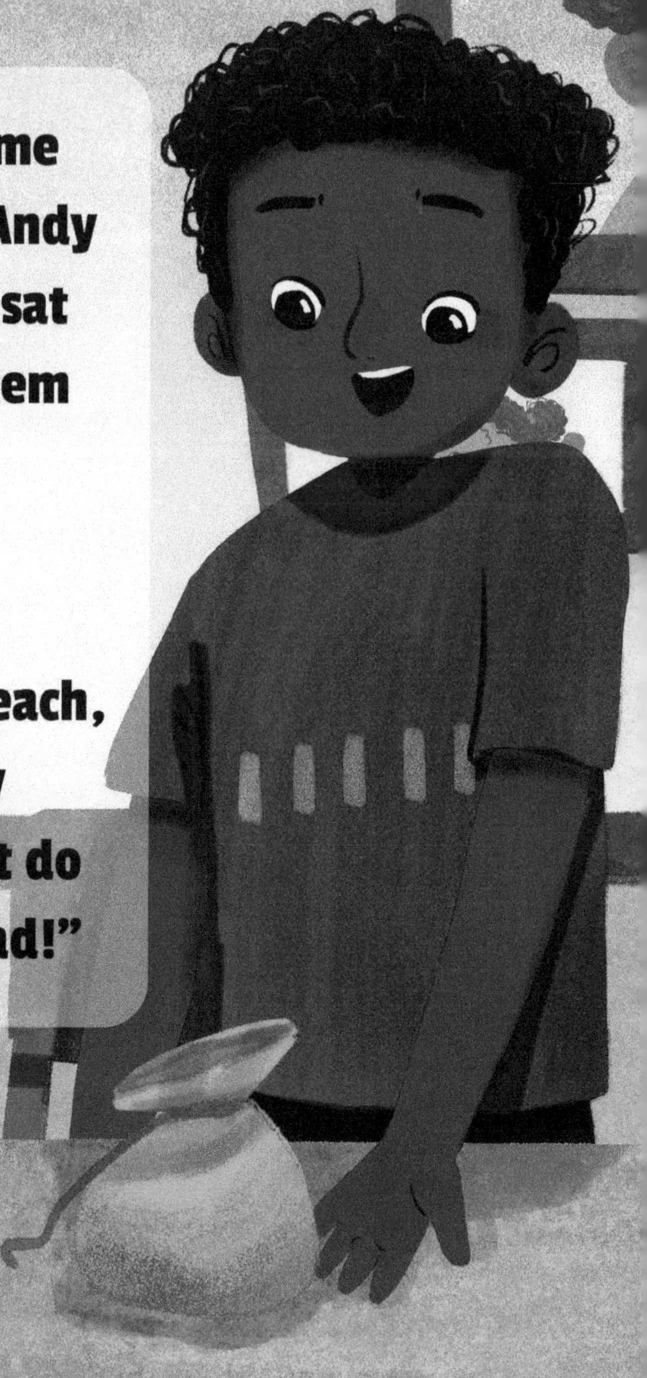

One day, Andy's dad brought home a bag of new candy and wanted Andy to taste it. After dinner, they all sat at the table. Dad gave each of them a piece.

"Wow!" Mom exclaimed.

"Yummy!" Jill squealed.

There were grape, strawberry, peach, vanilla, chocolate, and blueberry flavors. Well, tell me Andy? What do you think?" It's the best ever, Dad!"

"Good. There are more flavors in the bag. Andy, take some to school tomorrow and see what your friends think."

The next day at school, Andy gave all his friends a piece. They were blown away. It was some of the best candy they had ever tasted.

Later at home, Andy's dad asked him if his friends liked the candy. "They sure did!" Andy smiled. It seemed like every five minutes, someone was asking for more candy.

Dad set a great, big bag of candy on the table. Inside were all different flavors. "You're the best!" Andy ran and gave Dad a big hug. "Yeah, I know." They all laughed.

Soon, it was bedtime. Mom tucked Jill and Andy in bed for the night. The next morning, Andy did his chores and played with Jill. Later that afternoon, Andy's friends came over to play for a while. "Can we have more candy, Andy?"

Here we go again, Andy thought as he gave them a piece.

Later that night, Dad had some bad news for everyone. The factor would not be giving out anymore free samples of the multi-flavored candy. They said it cost too much to make. He gave Andy the last bag of candy. It was bigger than all the others.

At school, all the kids were trying to get to Andy for some more of his delicious candy. Andy managed to get away that day, but the next day, Sarah asked him if she could have a piece. “Maybe later,” Andy told her.
“Aww, come on, Andy,” she begged.
“I know you have enough. Meet me on the playground at recess, ok?” “Alright,” Andy sighed.

Just as he started to walk away, Steve popped up. “How about some more of that candy,” he asked holding out his hand. “I’m not sure, Steve. I only have a little left.” “Come on, Andy! I’m your best friend,” Steve threw up his hands. Soon, a large crowd of kids had gathered around Andy.

“Okay. Everyone meet me on the playground at recess,” Andy said as he managed to break through the crowd.

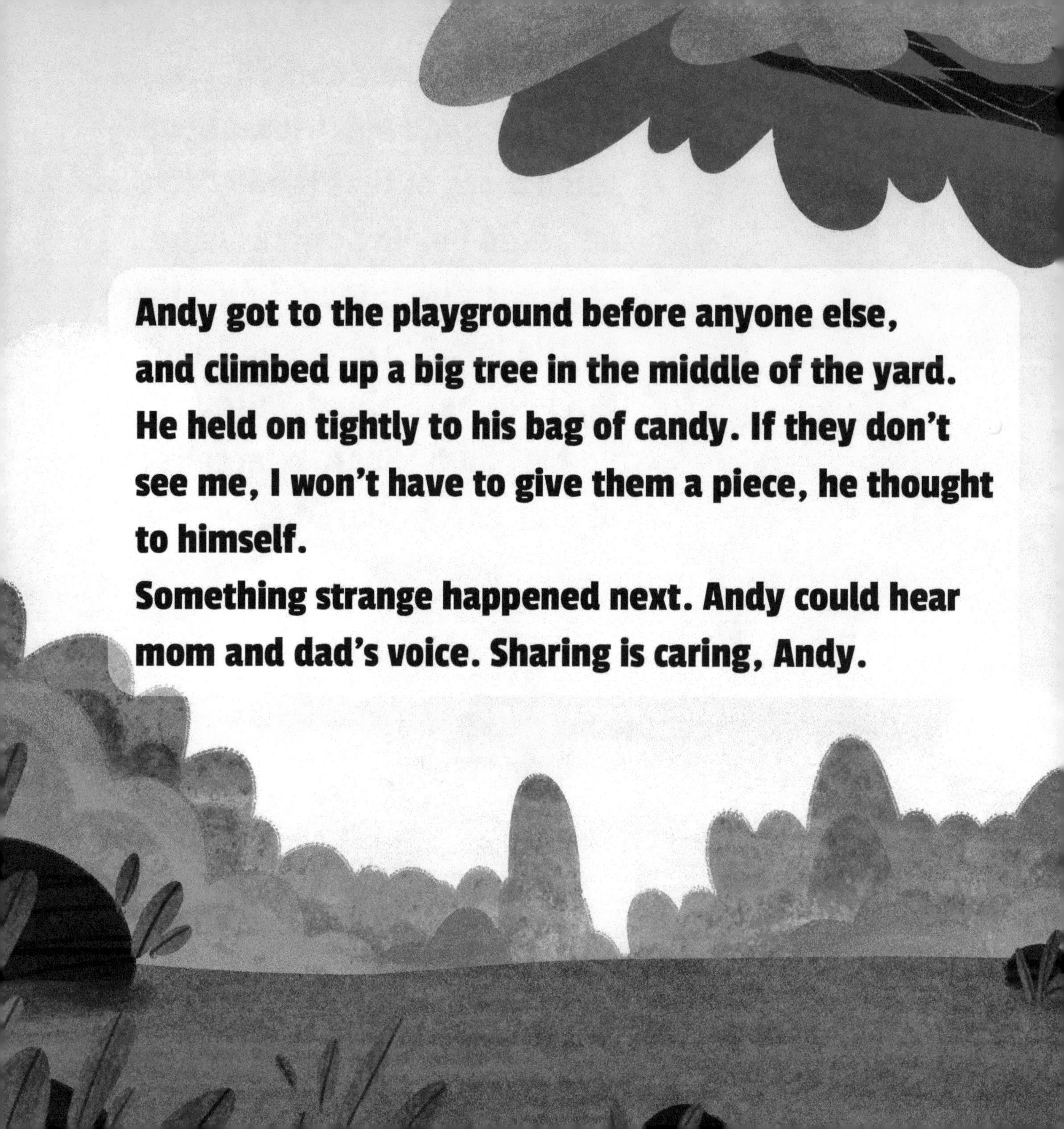

Andy got to the playground before anyone else, and climbed up a big tree in the middle of the yard. He held on tightly to his bag of candy. If they don't see me, I won't have to give them a piece, he thought to himself.

Something strange happened next. Andy could hear mom and dad's voice. Sharing is caring, Andy.

Yep, that was them alright, but there was no one but Andy up in the tree.

The bell rang and all the kids ran out onto the playground. “Where’s Andy?” they all asked.

They all began to search under the sliding board, in between the swings, and inside the Jungle Gym.

Andy watched everything from high up in the tree. He began to feel bad, but this was the only way he didn't have to share. Andy began to move down to get a better look, and slipped! His bag of candy ripped opened and fell to the ground.

"Look!" someone screamed.

"It's raining candy!"

All the kids scrambled over to the tree and began picking up all the pieces of rainbow colored candy.

Sarah looked up and spotted Andy in the tree. "Andy Dandy, what are you doing up there? Come down right now!"

Andy was pretty sad practically all his candy was gone, but he was thankful not all of it fell out of the bag. Andy saw how happy the other kids were. It was some of the best candy in the world.

After recess, Andy kept thinking about this being the last batch of candy. No more!?! All the kids were talking about what happened, so much so, even some of the teachers got wind of it.

Miss Baker, the math teacher, thought it was a good idea to let Andy's mom know what happened, too. She decided to give her a call. Mom told dad, and dad told everyone at the candy factory. They all had a good laugh about Andy's latest adventure.

Meanwhile, the school was planning the big end of the year field trip. During dinner that night, Andy and Jill talked about places they'd like to go.

Sprinkleville Zoo and the children's museum were class favorites, but Andy thought it would be fun to go somewhere different this year.

"Well," started Dad, "everyone at the candy factory did say I could bring you kids in for a tour-"

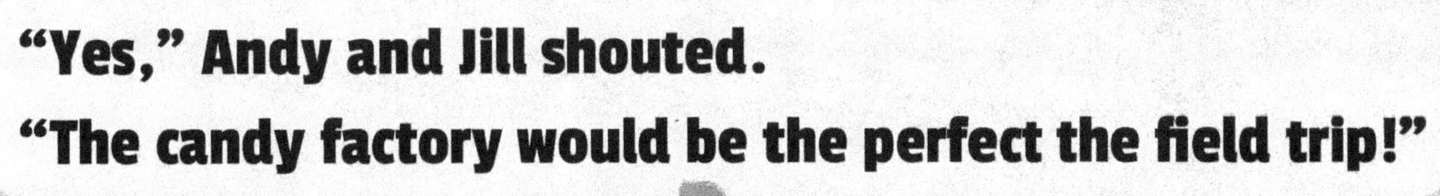

"Yes," Andy and Jill shouted.

"The candy factory would be the perfect the field trip!"

"Slow down, guys," Dad said.
"I said you and Jill, not the entire school.
I'd have to clear this with management first."

The next day, Andy could hardly wait for his dad to come home from work. “So what did they say?” Andy asked Dad let out a big sigh. “Well, Andy.”

“Come on dad, tell me!”

“They said yes! Your class is welcomed to visit for the entire day. My boss is calling the school principal to work out the details!”

The day of the field trip was the best! They were able to see how all the candy for Sprinkleville is made. As they were leaving, everyone was able to take home a bag of candy!

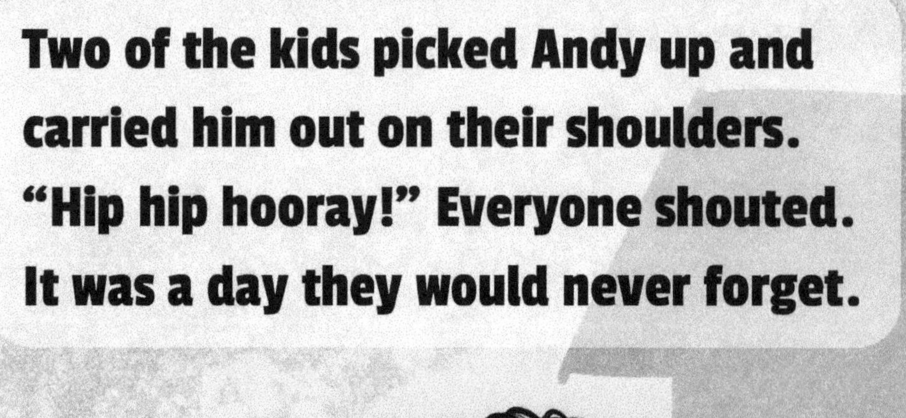

Two of the kids picked Andy up and carried him out on their shoulders. "Hip hip hooray!" Everyone shouted. It was a day they would never forget.

NDY

About the Author

William N. Savage creates heart-warming, humorous, literary adventures for children of all ages. His love of oral story-telling began at a young age in his hometown of Bonneau, South Carolina, where he learned to put a creative spin on small town upbringing. As a former truck driver and statewide "Mr. Fix It," William's time on the open road ignited many creative stories rooted in memories of that small town life in the low country.

William's stories would soon evolve to include the adventures of his five children as they grew. His stories are special, as he and his three older sisters were raised by their grandparents who passed on the true value of unconditional love and respect for others. William appreciates all his grandparents did for him, calling them a "true blessing." His other talents include repairing broken items, telling jokes, baking the world's best sweet potato pies, and making up silly songs. People call him a jack-of-all-trades, but he will be the first to tell you he would trade all his jacks just to tell his grandparents he loves them again. So, he makes sure his entire family hears this daily.

Nowadays, William resides in Columbia, South Carolina, with his two youngest children. Email him at willsav63@aol.com.

"Sharing is caring!"
- Andy

CPSIA information can be obtained
at www.ICGtesting.com
Printed in the USA
BVHW021516161121
621776BV00022B/785